Copyright © 2001 by Nord-Süd Verlag AG, Gossau Zürich, Switzerland
First published in Switzerland under the title *Teddy feiert Halloween*.
English translation copyright © 2001 by North-South Books Inc.
All rights reserved. No part of this book may be reproduced or
utilized in any form or by any means, electronic or mechanical, including
photocopying, recording, or any information storage and retrieval
system, without permission in writing from the publisher.

First published in the United States, Great Britain, Canada,
Australia, and New Zealand in 2001 by North-South Books,
an imprint of Nord-Süd Verlag AG, Gossau Zürich, Switzerland.
Distributed in the United States by North-South Books Inc., New York.

Library of Congress Cataloging-in-Publication Data is available.
A CIP catalogue record for this book is available from The British Library.
ISBN 0-7358-1530-5 (trade binding)
1 3 5 7 9 TB 10 8 6 4 2
ISBN 0-7358-1531-3 (library binding)
1 3 5 7 9 LB 10 8 6 4 2
Printed in Belgium

For more information about our books, and the authors and artists
who create them, visit our web site: www.northsouth.com

Teddy's Halloween Secret

By Gerlinde Wiencirz

Illustrated by Giuliano Lunelli

Translated by J. Alison James

North-South Books
New York · London

At last it was Halloween, the day Paul had been waiting for. "Yippie!" he cried as he tossed Teddy in the air. "Tonight is my party! Everyone is invited, but nobody can come without a costume!" He hugged Teddy to his chest and whispered, "Guess what my costume is? I'm going to be the devil king!"

   Paul was very busy getting ready for his party. He had to carve the pumpkins. He had to try on his costume. He had to paint his face.

   Teddy wanted to go to the party, too. But how could he? He didn't have a costume. When Paul went into the bathroom, Teddy slipped out the back door, across the garden, and ran into the woods.

Down by the big fir tree lived his friend, the little rabbit. Teddy told him about the Halloween party.

"Oh what fun!" Rabbit cried. "What do you want to be?"

"Anything," Teddy said. "I just can't look like me."

"Well, let's start with some rabbit ears," Rabbit said, and quickly he went to work. He giggled when he tried them on Teddy. "Perfect," Rabbit said. "But you need something more. Let's ask Owl."

The two of them ran to Owl's tree. She was fast asleep.
Teddy and Rabbit shouted, "Owl, Owl, wake up!"

"What's all the fuss?" Owl asked, blinking sleepily.

Teddy told her about the Halloween party.

"Oh, what fun!" Owl hooted. "What do you want to be?"

"Anything," said Teddy. "I just can't look like me."

"Here, take my sunglasses, then nobody will see your
button eyes."

"Thank you, Owl!" cried Teddy, and he put them on.

"Perfect," said Rabbit. "But you need something more.
Let's ask Fox."

But there in the grass was Mouse. "Excuse me," she said. "I heard you calling for help. Sometimes even a mouse can help."

"Thank you," said Teddy, and he told her about the Halloween party.

"Oh, what fun!" Mouse squeaked. "What do you want to be?"

"Anything," said Teddy. "I just can't look like me."

"I know, you can put a few of my whiskers on your nose."

"Thank you, Mouse!" cried Teddy, and he put them on.

"Perfect," said Rabbit. "But you need something more."

Teddy was a little nervous when he told Fox about the Halloween party.

But the fox laughed out loud. "Oh, what fun!" he howled. "What do you want to be?"

"Anything," said Teddy. "I just can't look like me."

"Well, my bushy tail has an extra tuft. You're welcome to it."

"Thank you, Fox," said Teddy. "I'll put it on my head tonight, just like a horn."

"Perfect," said Rabbit. "But you need something more."

"I could show you to the hen house," offered Fox, "and get you a few feathers."

Rabbit laughed. "We know the way. But thanks for the idea."

Teddy told the hens about the Halloween party.

"Oh, what fun!" they cackled. "What do you want to be?"

"Anything," said Teddy. "I just can't look like me."

"Well, we've got enough feathers for a coat!" The hens shook up a storm of feathers, and Rabbit made them into a coat. Then he stood back from Teddy and looked.

"Perfect," Rabbit said. "Nobody will know you now!"

It had grown dark. The party had already started. Teddy could hear laughing and shrieking as shadows danced by the windows. Teddy rang the bell. The Devil King himself answered the door, and his friends swarmed behind him.

"Who is it?" they cried. "We thought everyone was here!" They all stopped and stared at Teddy.

"What kind of creature is that?" they asked. "Who are you? Do we know you? What's your name?"

Then Paul stepped up and said, "This is the best costume yet. Let the bunny-bird join the party. We'll find out who it is soon enough."

So they started to dance again, and played party games. Teddy was having a wonderful time.

When the clock struck seven, the Devil King clapped his hands. "Time to go trick-or-treating!" he said.

The children took their jack-o'-lanterns and headed out.
They ran house to house, crying, "trick or treat, trick or treat,
give us something good to eat!" Soon their sacks were full
of sweets.

On the way back to Paul's house, Teddy lagged behind the others.

"Hurry up," called the children.

"I'll be right there," Teddy called back.

He waited until all the children had gone back inside the house then ran as fast as lightning through the back garden and disappeared into the night.

All the animals were waiting by the great fir tree. They were so excited to hear what had happened that the mouse lay down by the fox, and the fox found himself chatting with the hens. But the little rabbit kept an eye on him, just in case.

Teddy told them all about his adventure. No one at the party had guessed who he was.

The animals laughed with delight.

Teddy thanked them again for their help, then he brought out his bag and shared his sweets among them all.

Paul didn't notice when Teddy slipped into bed just before dawn. And he never found out that the mysterious bunny-bird had been his very own Teddy!